W9-BST-368

Where Are You?

For Kate Burns - with thanks
F.S.

For my mother and in memory
of my father
D.M.

Published by
PEACHTREE PUBLISHERS, LTD.
494 Armour Circle NE
Atlanta, Georgia 30324

Text © 1998 by Francesca Simon
Illustrations © 1998 by David Melling

First published by Hodder Children's Books, a division of Hodder Headline plc, in Great Britain in 1998.

First United States edition by Peachtree Publishers, Ltd., in September 1998.

Printed in Belgium

10 9 8 7 6 5 4 3 2 1
First Edition

Library of Congress Cataloging-in-Publication Data

Simon, Francesca.
    Where are you? / Francesca Simon : [illustrations by] David Melling --1st ed.
        p.   cm.
    Summary : When Harry and his grandfather go to the grocery store, Harry races off to follow the wonderful smells and gets lost.
    ISBN 1-56145-179-7
    [1. Grocery shopping--Fiction.   2. Shopping--Fiction.
3. Grandfathers--Fiction.   4. Lost children--Fiction.   5. Dogs--Fiction.]
    I. Melling, David, ill.   II. Title.
    PZ7.S604Wk   1998
    [E]--dc21   97-52586
                                  CIP
                                  AC

Where Are You?

Francesca Simon • David Melling

PEACHTREE

ATLANTA

One day, Harry and Grandpa
went to the supermarket.
Harry had never been in such
a wonderful place before.

Suddenly Harry sniffed the most delicious smell.

"Yum . . . cupcakes!" said Harry.

ZIP!

Off he went.

"We need apples," said Grandpa.
"We need pizza."
"We need . . .

"Harry? Harry? Where are you?"

"He's not under the bananas."

"He's not under the lettuce."

"He's not under the beans."

"Ah, there you are, Harry!" said Grandpa.
"What are you doing up there?"

SNATCH!

"Oops!" said Grandpa. "Pardon me.
Have you seen Harry?"

"Hey!" said Mrs. Ruffle. "He went that-a-way."
"Harry! Where are you?" said Grandpa.

Harry was on the cupcake trail.

"Cold," said Harry. "BRRRR!"

"Dark," said Harry.
"OOOH!"

"Slippery," said Harry.
"WHEEEE!"

He was getting closer to the cupcakes.

"Harry! Where are you?" said Grandpa.

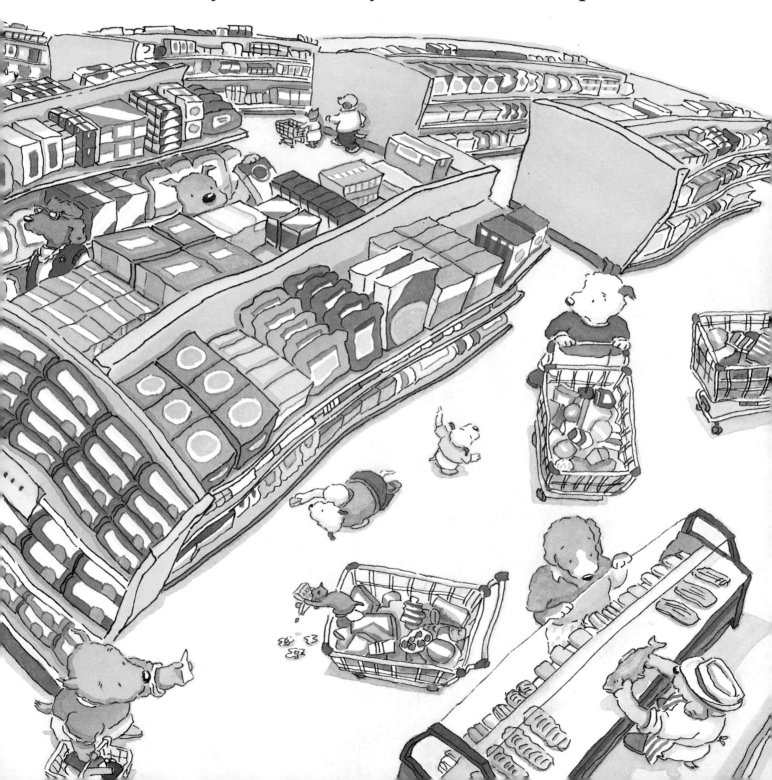

Then Harry saw the cupcakes.

"We need cupcakes, Grandpa,"
said Harry.

"Grandpa?"

Harry stopped.

"You're not Grandpa.
You're not Grandpa."
Then suddenly . . .

"There you are, Grandpa!" said Harry.

"Oh no! You're not Grandpa!
GRANDPA! WHERE ARE YOU?"

"HARRY! WHERE ARE YOU?"

CRASH!

"You were lost, Grandpa," said Harry.
"You were lost, Harry," said Grandpa.

"But now we're found."

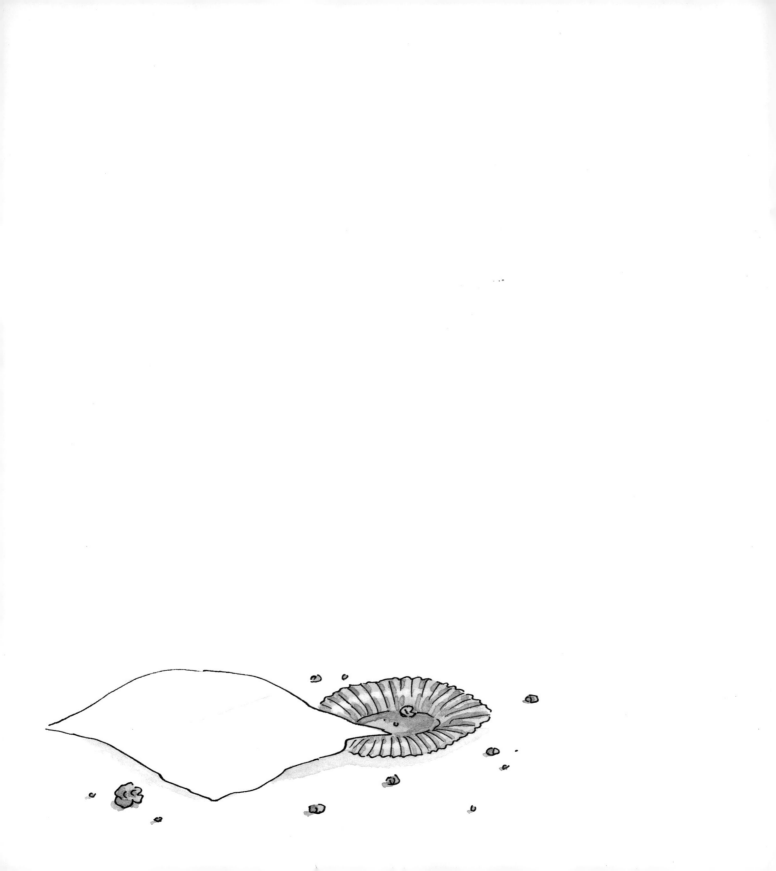